KB086025

트렁크

도서출판 아시아에서는 《바이링궐 에디션 한국 현대 소설》을 기획하여 한국의 우수한 문학을 주제별로 엄선해 국내외 독자들에게 소개합니다. 이 기획은 국내외 우수한 번역가들이 참여하여 원작의 품격을 최대한 살렸습니다. 문학을 통해 아시아의 정체성과 가치를 살피는 데 주력해 온 도서출판 아시아는 한국인의 삶을 넓고 깊게 이해하는 데 이 기획이 기여하기를 기대합니다.

Asia Publishers present some of the very best modern Korean literature to readers worldwide through its new Korean literature series 〈Bi-lingual Edition Modern Korean Literature〉. We are proud and happy to offer it in the most authoritative translation by renowned translators of Korean literature. We hope that this series helps to build solid bridges between citizens of the world and Koreans through rich in-depth understanding of Korea.

바이링궐 에디션 한국 현대 소설 025

Bi-lingual Edition Modern Korean Literature 025

In the Trunk

정이현

트렁크

Jeong Yi-hyun

ASIA
PUBLISHERS

Contents

트렁크

In the Trunk

토요일 오후 네 시

그녀는 모든 것이 꿈이라고 확신했다.

아침부터 흩날리던 가느다란 눈발이 어느 순간 함박눈이 되어 쏟아지고 있었다. 와이퍼가 고장인지 빠르게 움직일 때마다 앞 유리창은 점점 더 뿌옇게 얼룩져 갔다. 트렁크 어디쯤 영업사원이 넣어둔 면걸레가 있을 터였다. 그녀는 비상등을 켜고 갓길에 차를 세웠다. 운전석 도어 밑의 레버를 당기면서 문득 이 차의 트렁크를 아직 한 번도 열어본 적 없다는 사실을 깨달았다. 하긴 그녀는 트렁크 가득 여행 가방을 싣고 놀러 다닐 만큼 한가한 사람은 못 되었다. 종이 박스째 청과물을 사들이는 경우도, 대형

Saturday, 4 p.m.

It had to be a dream.

Before she knew it, the morning's snow flurries had thickened into large flakes. She wondered if something was wrong with the windshield wipers—when she set them on high, the windshield only fogged up more. There had to be a hand towel somewhere, one of the little extras to remember the dealer by. Maybe in the trunk? She turned on her hazard blinkers and pulled over. As she reached down and popped the lid she realized she hadn't seen the inside of it yet. Well, so what? She didn't have the leisure to be gallivanting about the coun-

화환을 운반하는 일도 없었다. 대부분의 운전자들처럼 거기, 트렁크가 따라오고 있다는 것도 의식하지 못한 채 앞만 보고 달렸다. 목덜미에 눈송이의 선뜩한 감촉이 느껴졌다. 그녀는 트렁크 덮개를 힘껏 들어올렸다.

그 안에 무언가가 있었다.

소녀는 동그랗게 몸을 만 채 옆으로 누워 있었다. 툭 어깨를 치면 금세라도 일어나 차장님! 하고 그녀를 부를 것만 같았다. 그녀는 멍하니 트렁크 안을 들여다보았다. 정수리 위에, 캐시미어 코트 위에, 가죽 부츠의 날렵한 코 위에 후득후득 눈발이 떨어졌다. 일기예보에도 없는 폭설이었다. 전조등을 밝힌 차들이 먹장구름 사이를 헤치고 획획 달렸다.

그녀는 가만히 트렁크를 닫았다. 운전석에 앉자 비로소 턱이 덜덜 떨려왔다.

한 달 전

이 나라에서 생산되는 2,000cc급 자동차는 네댓 종류뿐이었다. 그녀는 각 자동차 회사의 대리점에 전화를 걸어 카탈로그와 제원표를 보내달라고 요청했다. 그녀가 차를 바꿀 계획이라는 소문은 지사(支社) 안에 쫙 퍼졌다. 원래

tryside. Nor did she need the trunk for cartons of produce for her table or mammoth wreaths for ceremonial occasions. She was like most drivers, focusing on what lay ahead.

She felt the chill of the snow flakes on the back of her neck as she flung open the lid. That's when she saw the shape. It was the girl. Curled up on her side. She felt an urge to tap the girl on the shoulder, hoping she'd startle, wake up, say *Oh, hello, ma'am.* Instead she could only gape at her. She felt flakes of snow coming to rest on her head, saw them gather on her cashmere coat and the tips of her leather boot. It wasn't supposed to snow this much. Cars sped by, headlights on, plunging into the inky gloom.

Gently she closed the trunk. It didn't hit her until she was back in the car—she started to shiver, her teeth clattering.

One Month Earlier

Back then you could count on the fingers of one hand the number of domestically produced cars equipped with two-liter engines. She had called the dealers, asking for brochures and specs. Once the word got out, everyone knew she was in the market

그런 곳이었다. 목례만 하고 지내던 물류팀 직원이 찾아와 카딜러인 매제를 소개해주겠다고 말했다. 그녀가 잠시 침묵하는 사이 그가 얼른 덧붙였다. 유능한 사람이에요. 지난 분기의 판매왕이었으니. 고마워요. 그러나 오래전부터 약속한 데가 있어서요. 그녀는 눈꼬리를 내려뜨리며 진심으로 아쉽다는 표정을 지었다. 이 녀석은 새 임자를 찾으셨나? 건물의 늙은 주차 관리원은 그녀가 사 년여째 타온 군청색 아반떼에 노골적으로 눈독을 들였다. 친구가 가져가겠다는데 걱정이에요. 겉보기만 멀쩡하지 잔고장이 많거든요. 천연한 말투에 중늙은이는 쩝, 입맛을 다셨다.

주간 스케줄은 촘촘히 조직되어 있었다. 그녀는 외근 핑계를 대고 개인적인 쇼핑을 하거나 심지어 아이 유치원의 재롱잔치에 참석하기까지 하는 여직원들을 경멸했다. 일요일, 장로교회의 오전 예배를 마치고 손톱 손질을 받으러 가는 길에 자동차 영업소를 방문했다. 영업사원은 아주 친절했다. 4단 자동 변속기와 우드 그레인, 크림색 가죽 시트가 포함된 옵션을 권유하면서 할부 기간에 따른 판매 조건을 조목조목 설명해주었다. 계약은 순조롭게 이루어졌다. 아반떼는 5백만 원 상당의 가치로 상환되었고,

for a new car—that's the kind of company she worked at. A guy from Distribution, someone she knew only in passing, had offered to introduce her to his brother-in-law car dealer. When she hesitated he was quick to add, *Top salesman last quarter—he knows what he's doing.* She thanked him, then said she'd already arranged to visit another dealership first—she'd tried to sound sincere, but had to break off eye contact before she finished. *You got someone in mind to saddle up this old pony?* The elderly parking garage attendant had asked her, eyeing the navy-blue Avante she'd been driving for the last four years. *One of my friends says he's interested,* she'd replied, but *I'm worried something's going to happen—it doesn't have a scratch, but there are all these little issues, you know? Too bad,* the man had tsk-tasked.

She was a woman who scheduled her week down to the last detail, and she despised the women who managed to disappear now and then on "company business" to go shopping or attend a function at their child's kindergarten. And so the visit to the dealership had to wait until Sunday, after the morning service at the Presbyterian church and before her appointment at the nail salon. The salesman

나머지 금액은 십이분의 일로 나뉘어 은행 계좌로부터 매달 자동 이체될 것이다. 새 차는 일주일 뒤에 도착했다. 옛 차에서 꺼낸 짐은 CD 몇 장과 볼펜, 휴대용 물티슈가 전부였다. 그녀는 대시보드 위에 알락달락한 십자수 쿠션이나 만화 캐릭터 모양의 플라스틱 방향제를 올려놓고 다니며 우스꽝스런 취향을 과시하는 사람들을 이해하지 못했다. 군더더기 없이 심플하게, 지금까지 그래왔던 것처럼 그녀는 새 차의 내부에 아무런 장식도 하지 않을 것이었다.

탁송인이 아반떼를 몰고 떠나자 그녀는 새 차와 단둘이 남겨졌다. 주거용 오피스텔의 지하 주차장은 대낮에도 어둑했다. 무선 도어 록의 버튼을 누르는 순간 탈칵, 소리와 함께 헤드라이트에 주황색 불빛이 명멸했다. 공업용 비닐로 덮인 실내에서는 차가운 금속과 덜 마른 페인트의 냄새가 났다. 조심스레 시동을 걸어보았다. 엔진 소리는 놀랄 만큼 부드러웠다. 대한민국에서 배기량 2,000cc급 자동차의 오너가 되는 것은 결코 만만한 일이 아니었다. 2002년형 진주색 EF 소나타 골드. 그녀는 자신의 새 차가 마음에 들었다.

was very attentive. He explained all the options—the four-speed automatic transmission, the wood-grain paneling, the cream-colored leather seats—and went over the various payment schedules. The signing of the sales contract went without a hitch—she would get five million for the Avante trade-in and pay the balance in twelve monthly auto-pay installments. Her new car was delivered a week later. All she had to salvage from the Avante were a few CDs, a pen, and a packet of hand-wipes. She couldn't understand the car owners who were so proud of the little cushion on their dashboard cross-stitched with their phone number. It was almost as stupid as the deodorizers in the shape of cartoon characters. No clutter in her life—consistent with this mantra, there would be no adornments to her car.

The delivery man drove off in the Avante, and there she was, alone with her new car. It was gloomy even in midday in the underground parking garage of the officetel where she lived. She pressed the keyless lock, heard a click from the doors, and the headlights came on, bright orange. The interior, clad in industrial-grade vinyl seat covers, had the new-car smell of metal and of paint that was not

금요일 오전 여섯 시

여느 때처럼 그녀는 여섯 시에 눈을 떴다. 지난밤 자정 뉴스에서 서울의 아침 기온 영하 삼 도, 대륙성 고기압의 영향으로 흐리고 구름 많은 전형적인 겨울 날씨가 될 것이라고 알려주었다. 미리 세운 플랜에 따라 목까지 단추를 채우는 화이트 셔츠와 감색 수트를 입고 막스마라의 연회색 캐시미어 코트를 걸쳤다. 반듯한 커리어 우먼으로 보이는 데에는 큼지막한 에르메스 가죽 백도 중요한 역할을 했다. 지난봄 석 달 동안 대기자 명단에 이름을 올린 끝에 구입한, 가장 아끼는 가방이었다. 겨울 외투나 핸드백, 브로치 같은 액세서리는 조금 무리를 하더라도 가능한 고급품으로 구입한다는 것이 그녀의 원칙이었다. 분당 집에서 대치동 회사까지는 도시고속화도로에 연결돼 있었다. 차에는 아무런 문제도 없어 보였다. 평균 시속 80km/h로 달려 오전 일곱 시 오 분경 강남에 진입했다. 회사 옆 피트니스 센터에서 웨이트 트레이닝과 간단한 샤워를 마친 시간은 여덟 시 이십오 분. 언제나처럼 그녀는 여덟 시 삼십 분경에 사무실에 들어섰다. 잔심부름을 하는 아르바이트생을 제외하고는 사무실 전체에서 제일 이른 출근이었다.

quite dry. Gingerly she tried the ignition. The purr of the engine was so quiet. In the Republic of Korea in the year 2002, not just anyone could acquire a two-liter car. Yes, her new pearl white Sonata Gold EF would do quite nicely.

Friday, 6 a.m.

As usual she woke up at six to the alarm clock. The weather forecast on the late-night news had called for typical winter weather—clouds, a high-pressure system from the mainland, and a temperature of minus 3 for the morning commute. She had laid out her outfit the night before—white high-neck, button-up blouse, indigo pants suit, light gray Maxmara cashmere coat. And, essential to the image of a Career Woman, her Hermes leather tote. She'd ordered it last spring, was on the waiting list three months before she received it, and now it was her favorite bag. Winter coats, accessories such as handbags and broaches—everything was top drawer. That was her policy when it came to outfitting herself, even though it sometimes strained her budget. The City Expressway connected the new urban enclave of Bundang, where she lived, with her workplace in the Daechi-dong area of Seoul. An

일찍 일어나는 새가 벌레를 잡는다는 고전적인 경구의 신봉자는 아니었으나 규정 시간보다 빠른 출근은 첫 직장에서부터 이어져오는 습관이었다. 조금만 서두르면 하루를 훨씬 여유 있게 시작하게 될 뿐더러 예기치 않은 것들까지 덤으로 알 수 있게 된다. 교육 담당 대리 최는 매장 판매원 출신답게 세속적 출세에 대한 강박이 있었는데 안타깝게도 주의력이 부족했다. 『초간단 비즈니스 영어회화』나 『성공을 부르는 이미지 마케팅』 따위의 제목도 간지러운 실용서들을 책상 서랍 속에 넣어 놓고는 열쇠도 채우지 않고 다녔다. 여자 대학을 갓 졸업한 홍보팀 막내 윤과 마케팅팀 실무 책임자 김 과장 사이의 비밀스런 연애는 꾸준히 지속되고 있었다. 김 과장 자리의 전화기에서 리다이얼 버튼을 누르면 액정 화면에는 십중팔구 윤의 휴대폰 번호가 떴다. 여덟 시 사십오 분이 되자 N화장품 한국 지사의 로컬 직원들이 하나둘 출근하기 시작했다. 그녀는 데스크톱 모니터에 눈을 박고 경제신문의 오늘자 뉴스레터를 찬찬히 읽어나갔다. 평화로운 아침이었다.

열 시에는 지사장 주재의 간부 회의가 있었다. 과장급 이상 각 팀의 책임자와 이사들을 포함하여 일고여덟을 넘지 않은 인원이 원탁에 둘러앉았다. 아르바이트생 소녀가

easy commute, especially with the new car. Eighty kilometers an hour would get her to Seoul a little after seven. Weight training and a quick shower at the fitness center near the office, and it would be 8:25. Then arrive at the Korea branch of N Cosmetics by 8:30, as she always did. Except for the part-time office girl, she was the first arrival.

Not that she subscribed to the notion of the early bird catching the worm—ever since her first job she'd arrived early for work. A little bit of hustle first thing in the morning was a small price to pay for getting the workday off to a relaxed start. And there were some unexpected benefits. For example, Choe, who trained the new hires, was obsessed with getting ahead in the firm and putting behind him his background as a retail clerk, but unfortunately for him he tended to be careless. Who in his right mind would leave his desk drawer unlocked, with his self-help books vulnerable to prying eyes? *Business English Made Easy, Manage Your Image for Success*—the titles alone made her want to gag. And the hush-hush romance between Yun, the baby of the Promotion Team, fresh out of women's college, and Kim, head of the Marketing Team, was progressing. If you pressed redial on Kim's desk phone,

쟁반 가득 머그잔을 날라왔다. 그녀는 얼른 의자에서 일어나 습습한 놀림으로 좌중에 잔을 돌렸다. 커피 심부름 때문에 회사 생활이 힘들다고 징징대는 여자들은 신물나게 많았다. 그러나 조직 생활의 마인드가 부족하다면 일찌감치 결혼 정보 회사에 가입하여 집에 들어앉는 편이 유익하다는 것이 그녀의 견해였다. 먼저 백화점별 어제의 매출액이 보고되었고, 곧이어 그녀가 신제품 런칭 행사의 진행 상황을 중간 브리핑했다. 이번 봄 시즌에 출시되는 새로운 고농축 에센스는 극동 지역을 겨냥한 N사의 야심작이었다. 브랜든의 입장에서는 처음으로 맞는 능력 검증 무대가 될 것이다. 그녀 역시 브랜든이 부임한 한 달 전부터 이번 프로젝트에 집중하는 중이었다. 문제는 다시 피부 탄력이다, 로 시작되는 보도자료도 직접 썼고 진행자의 섭외와 디엠 발송, 행사장의 구체적인 인테리어까지, 그녀가 일일이 챙겨야 할 일은 무척 많았다. 젊은 CEO답게 브랜든은 그녀의 보고 중간중간 고개를 끄덕여 호응했으며 멋진 파티를 기대하겠다는 말로 코멘트를 대신했다. 브랜든 옆자리의 권은 회의가 끝날 때까지 단 한 차례도 입을 열지 않았다. 얼굴의 왼쪽 근육을 찌푸린 그의 표정이 고장난 트랜지스터라디오처럼 완강해 보여서 그녀는

Yun's cell phone number was almost certain to pop up on the display. At 8:45, when the others began to trickle in, she would already be at her desk, eyes glued to her monitor, following the online edition of that day's *Economy.* Another peaceful easy morning.

At ten o'clock on this particular morning the Branch Manager met with her and the rest of his staff, the seven or eight individuals who were either directors or team leaders. The office girl appeared with a tray loaded with mugs of coffee. She quickly rose and distributed them. She was sick of hearing the others whine about how tough it was working at a company where they had to serve the coffee. The women with that mindset should do everyone a favor and disappear—join one of the singles registries, get married, and settle down. After yesterday's sales figures at the various department stores were handed out, she gave a progress report on the launch of the super-concentrated essence to be unveiled that spring, N Cosmetics' high hope for the East Asia market. From Brandon's point of view, this event would be his screen test as new Branch Manager. And so this launch, a project Brandon had assigned her a month ago, required all of her con-

권태롭게 고개를 돌렸다.

금요일 오후 여섯 시

패션지의 뷰티 에디터와 막 통화를 끝냈을 때 윤이 그녀 곁으로 다가왔다. 차장님, 별일 없으면 저 먼저 들어가 볼게요. 윤은 벌써 어깨에 목도리를 두른 채 손에는 코트와 가방을 들고 있었다. 여섯 시가 좀 넘었을 뿐인데도 창밖엔 검푸른 어둠이 짙게 깔려 있었다. 직장 생활 구 년 차, 그녀는 까탈스런 상사는 아니었다. 먼저 갑니다. 김이었다. 윤이 나간 후 오 분도 지나지 않았다. 그녀는 짧게 올려 깎은 김의 뒤통수를 바라보면서 진지하게 한번 조언해주어야 하지 않을까 생각하다 그만두었다. 당사자만 모르는 공공연한 비밀은 어느 조직에나 존재하기 마련이었다. 약속 시간까지는 여유가 있었다. 그녀는 화장품 파우치를 들고 사무실을 나왔다. 여자 화장실에는 아무도 없었다. 두루마리 휴지를 양변기 주위에 돌려 깐 후 걸터앉아 화장을 고쳤다. 기름종이로 콧등과 이마를 꾹꾹 누르고 압축 파우더를 정성껏 두드려 발랐다. 쌍꺼풀 위에는 사파이어색 아이섀도를, 입술에는 자줏빛 립스틱을 덧칠했다. 타사키 지니아의 진주 목걸이와 귀고리 세트는 차

centration. The amount of detail was enormous, from the advertising copy, which she had written herself ("Once again it's all about the skin," it began), to the cast of characters at the launch, the direct mail campaign, and the site decor. Young CEO that he was, Brandon merely nodded in agreement during her briefing and concluded by saying he looked forward to the festive occasion. Kwon, sitting next to him, said not a word the whole time. Lately he'd been wearing an obstinate scowl that was especially pronounced on the left side of his face. She found it tiresome and tried to avoid looking at him.

Friday, 6 p.m.

She had just gotten off the phone with the Beauty editor of the fashion magazine when Yun came up to her, muffler about her neck, coat and handbag in hand. *Ma'am, would you mind if I left early?* It was shortly after six, but already blue-black dusk hung heavy outside the windows. For someone who had worked at a company for nine years, she wasn't that fussy a manager. The next to check out was Kim— *I'm off.* Not even five minutes had passed since Yun's departure. She thought for a moment as she

안에서 착용할 것이었다. 금요일 밤이었고 새로 생긴 차이니스 레스토랑을 방문할 예정이었으니, 그 정도의 치장은 당연했다.

화장실 앞에서 권과 마주쳤다. 우뚝 선 그를 비껴 지나려는 찰나 권이 그녀의 팔꿈치를 세게 붙잡았다. 핸드폰을 왜 꺼두었지? 요즘 그는 지나치게 예민했다. 그녀는 나직하게 대꾸했다. 배터리 충전을 잊었어. 웃기지 마. 네가 그런 실수를 할 사람이야? 권은 늙은 호랑이처럼 그르렁거리고 있었다. 기다릴게. 빨리 나와. 그녀는 뒤를 돌아보지 않고 총총 자리로 돌아갔다. 컴퓨터 네트워크를 종료하고 책상 서랍을 열쇠로 잠근 다음 천천히 코트를 입었다. 쓸데없이 상황이 복잡해지는 것은 싫었다. 넓은 사무실 안에는 남아 있는 사람이 많지 않았다. 그녀는 출입문 입구에 앉은 아르바이트생 소녀에게 다가갔다. 여자아이는 책상에 엎드리다시피 고개를 수그린 채 무언가에 열중하고 있었다. 선미 씨, 바쁜가 봐? 소녀가 의자에서 발딱 일어났다. 책상 위에는 양 손바닥만 한 다이어리가 펼쳐져 있었다. 하트나 나비 모양의 스티커를 다닥다닥 오려 붙이고 맨 앞 장엔 동글납작한 글씨로 연탄재 함부로 차지 마라, 같은 시구를 적어 놓았을 것이다. 그녀는 다정한

24

glanced at the back of Kim's closely cropped head that maybe she ought to offer them a word of friendly advice, but immediately thought better of it—every company had its open secrets, secrets as far as the principals were concerned, but common knowledge to everyone else. With time to spare before her dinner engagement, she left to fix her makeup. There was no one in the women's room. Draping tissue around the toilet seat, she perched herself there and got to work. She dabbed with an oil-absorbing sheet at the bridge of her nose and her forehead, then diligently patted on cake powder. Next the sapphire eye shadow above her double-lidded eyes, and a touch-up of her plum-colored lipstick. The pearl necklace and studs—her Tasaki Zenia set, adornments suitable for a Friday night dinner at a brand-new Chinese restaurant—could wait until the car.

Kwon had posted himself outside the bathroom. When she tried to get around him, he grabbed her by the arm. *Why aren't you answering?* He was so sensitive these days. *Sorry, I forgot to recharge*, she murmured, her tone impassive. *You forgot? Don't make me laugh*, Kwon growled. *Hurry up—I'll be waiting*. Without a backward look she scurried to

큰언니처럼 소녀의 어깨를 짚었다. 우리 같이 나가요. 추운데 전철역까지 태워다줄게. 권의 구형 볼보는 옥외 주차장 입구에 세워져 있었다. 선미는 자꾸 몇 발짝 뒤에서 따라왔다. 그녀는 걸음을 멈추고 소녀를 기다렸다. 권의 자동차 바로 앞에서 자연스레 선미의 팔짱을 끼었다.

　금요일 퇴근 시간답게 차가 많이 막혔다. 권이 따라오지 않는다는 것은 룸미러로 확인했다. 복잡한 주차장 같은 도로에서 무작정 쫓아오기란 쉽지 않을 것이다. 더구나 그는 남의 이목을 충분히 두려워할 줄 아는 사람이었다. 차장님, 차 진짜 좋아요. 소녀의 목소리가 너무 진지해서 조금 웃음이 났다. 그러고 보니 새 차를 뽑은 지 한 달이 되도록 이토록 직접적인 칭찬을 들은 건 처음이었다. 이 차, 괜찮아요? 작년에 제일 많이 팔렸다 그러더라구. 동료들은 대부분 객관적 데이터 뒤에 숨어 말하곤 했다. 그녀는 대답 대신 핸들 중간의 오디오 파워 버튼을 눌렀다. 안드레아 보첼리의 콘 테 파르티로(Con te Partiro)가 흘러나왔다. 차장님은 좋으시겠어요. 소녀의 한숨 소리는 음악에 묻혀 잘 들리지 않았다. 늘 이렇게 혼자 다닐 수 있어서. 그녀는 타인에게 항상 겸손한 편이었다. 좋긴 뭐가 좋아, 이렇게 차가 막히는데? 소녀가 헤헤 웃었다. 컬

her desk. Powered down her desktop, locked her drawer, then took her time putting on her coat. She hated it when things got complicated for no good reason. By now the large, open office was practically empty. She approached the office girl, sitting at her desk near the door, hunched over, wrapped up in something or other. *Hard at work, Seon-mi?* The girl jumped to attention. On the desk was her open diary, about the size of a pair of cupped palms. She imagined the pages festooned with stickers of hearts and butterflies, the writing round and squat, "Don't kick the ashes, don't make a mess" or some such saying jotted down on the first page. She placed a sisterly hand on the girl's shoulder. *How about a ride to the subway—it's cold out there.* Kwon was waiting in the parking lot in his old Volvo. Seon-mi kept lagging behind. She waited till the girl caught up with her, then, right in front of Kwon, nonchalantly linked arms with her.

The street was a virtual parking lot, par for the course during Friday rush hour. She looked in the mirror, didn't see Kwon's car. It wouldn't be easy to follow her unless he knew where she was going. And he was smart enough not to be obvious in his intentions. *Ma'am, this is a really cool car.* She had

러 프린터나 복사기처럼 조용히 시키는 일만 하는 아이인
줄 알았는데 밖에서 보니 아직 어린 태가 많이 났다. 저
나이 때 자신은 어떤 웃음소리를 갖고 있었던가. 잘 기억
나지 않았다.

첫 직장은 성형외과 병원이었다. 대학 취업 보도실에
붙은 공문은 대개 군필을 명기하고 있었고 그 외에는 중
학생 보습 학원의 시간 강사 자리가 다였다. 병원 면접을
보던 날 압구정동에 처음 가보았다. 당락을 결정하는 사
람은 원장 사모였다. 자연산인데 라인이 참 깔끔하게 떨
어졌네. 토익이나 워드 자격증이 아니라 쌍꺼풀 때문에
직장을 얻게 되리라고는 짐작도 못 했었지만 어쨌든 당시
엔 일자리를 구했다는 사실 자체에 안도했다. 그곳에서
그녀는 연분홍색 가운에 코디네이터라고 새긴 앙증맞은
명찰을 달고서, 고객들이 원하는 부위의 시술 금액과 할
인 혜택을 알려주는 일로 팔 개월을 보냈다. 그뒤에 썼던
어떤 이력서에도 그 시절의 경력을 굳이 밝히지는 않았
다. 조수석을 돌아보았다. 무턱대고 길게 길러 포니테일
로 묶은 머리, 군데군데 보푸라기가 일어난 더플 코트와
가짜 프라다 백팩. 다시 그 나이로 돌아가라면 그녀는 단
호히 고개를 저을 것이다.

to laugh, the girl was so unaffected. It occurred to her that this was the first direct compliment she'd heard in the month since she'd gotten the car. If it was one of her co-workers, it would have been something like, *How do you like that car? I read it was last year's top seller.* Most of them preferred to cite statistics rather than voice their own opinions. Instead of replying to the girl, she turned on the CD player. Out came the voice of Bocelli singing "Con te Partiro." *Lucky you, ma'am, you get to go anywhere you want,* the girl sighed, her voice almost lost in the music. *Me, lucky? Lucky to be stuck in traffic?* Respectful and gently indulgent as always. The girl giggled. She had thought of the girl as an automaton, going about her chores with all the quiet efficiency of a Xerox machine, but here outside the office she could see there was still a lot of the young girl about her. She tried in vain to remember what her own laughter had sounded like when she was Seon-mi's age.

Her first job had been at a cosmetic surgery clinic. The job listings posted on campus were mostly for the male students who had completed their compulsory military service before graduating. Or else postings for instructors at junior-high cram schools. The

벌써 몇 분째 차는 꿈쩍도 하지 않고 있었다. 자기는 꿈이 뭐야? 제 입에서 느닷없이 왜 그런 소리가 나왔는지 그녀도 알 수 없었다. 꿈 없어? 사람은 희망을 가져야 돼. 하긴 그 나이엔 그걸 알 턱이 없지. 그때 앞 차가 갑자기 움직이기 시작했다. 감사합니다, 차장님. 공손히 인사를 하고 소녀가 지하철 역 계단 아래로 사라졌다. 그녀는 교통방송으로 채널을 바꿨다. 이쪽 길로 들어서지 않았다면 퇴근길 정체를 피할 수 있었을지도 몰랐다. 남부순환로 양재에서 예술의 전당 방면 가나 시다 빈복하고 있고 반대편 양재 쪽으로도 지체 계속되고 있습니다. 자, 다음은 고속도로 정보 알려주세요. 약속 시간까지는 이십 분도 채 남아 있지 않았다. 브랜든은 저녁 데이트에 지각하는 여자를 귀여워할 타입은 아니었다. 그녀는 서둘러 액셀러레이터를 밟았다.

금요일 오후 일곱 시 반

브랜든은 음식에 만족해 했다. 오품 냉채와 삭스핀 수프, 간장소스의 은대구 튀김과 안심 구이가 들어 있는 코스였다. 소호에 자주 가던 차이니스 바가 있어요. 옆 테이블에 마크 제이콥스가 앉아 있어도 아무도 쳐다보지 않죠,

clinic was in Apgujeong-dong, a part of Seoul she had never been to. Her fate would be decided by the clinic director's wife. *Nice eyes, the outlines are perfect, and they're* natural. She'd never dreamed she would be hired on the basis of her double eyelids rather than her TOEIC score or her proficiency with software. But at the time, nine years ago, she was relieved simply to land a job. She'd lasted eight months there, wearing a light pink version of a doctor's whites and a tiny name tag that read *Coordinator*, advising clients of the per-facial-feature or per-body-part fees and the various payment plans, some of which came with a discount. That first job didn't appear on any of her subsequent resumes. She glanced at the girl. Her hair was in a ponytail grown wild. Little balls of fabric were showing on her duffle coat, and her student backpack was a Prada knock-off. No way would she relive that period of her life.

For the umpteenth time the car came to a standstill. *What would you like to be?* she asked the girl. And then, asking herself why she'd blurted the question, she followed up with, *Everybody has a dream, right? Something they're hoping for? Well, you'll know soon enough.* And then they were mov-

나중에 같이 가봐요. 그녀는 제 몫의 음식 접시를 깨끗이 비웠다. 처음에 서울에 온다고 생각했을 때는, 음, 솔직히 걱정했어요. 하지만 지금은 여기에 오길 아주 잘했다고 생각해요, 아주. 브랜든은 한국어의 부사(副詞)를 다양하게 구사하지 못한다. 아주, 라는 말을 반복하는 것으로 보아 그것은 그의 진심임이 틀림없었다. 그렇다면 정말 다행이네요. 지사장님이 오신 다음부터 확실히 분위기가 달라졌어요. 뭐랄까, 훨씬 활기 있어졌죠. 브랜든이 서클 렌즈를 낀 그녀의 눈동자를 똑바로 응시했나.

브랜든이 계산을 하는 동안 그녀는 화장실로 가 방금 먹은 음식을 모두 토했다. 십오 년째 웨이스트 사이즈 26을 유지한다는 건 보기보다 성가시고 어려운 일이었다. 공들여 양치를 하고 립스틱을 다시 바른 다음 휴대전화의 음성 메시지를 확인했다. 세 개 모두 권의 목소리였다. 그 새끼랑 있는 건 아니지?…… 내가 안 된다고 분명히 말했을 텐데…… 올 때까지 기다릴게. 요사이 권은 예민한 데다 극도로 유치해져가기까지 했다. 권의 내심을 모르는 건 아니었다. 그는 자신의 서포트가 없었다면 그녀가 지금의 직함을 갖는 데 훨씬 더 많은 시간이 소요되었으리라고 믿고 있었다. 어쨌든 지난 오 년 동안 사적으로나 공

ing again. *Thank you, ma'am*, said the girl before disappearing down the steps to the subway. She switched on the traffic channel, wondering if she could have saved time by taking a different route. *The south-river loop is stop-and-go from Yangjae to the National Arts Center, and coming the other way we have slowdowns approaching Yangjae. As for the expressways...* She checked the time—less than twenty minutes—and stepped on the gas. Brandon wouldn't appreciate a dinner date showing up late.

Friday, 7:30 p.m.

Brandon was pleased with the meal—a quintet of cold appetizers followed by Sharksfin soup, deep-fried sablefish in soy dressing, and beef tenderloin. *There's this Chinese bar I go to in Soho. You might have Marc Jacobs sitting next to you, but nobody pays any attention. We should go there sometime.* She finished all of her portions. *When I learned I was assigned to Seoul, well, to be honest, I was worried. But now that I'm here I think it was a great move—great.* Brandon's Korean was skimpy on adverbs. But great came out so often she had no doubt he was sincere. *That's wonderful. The atmosphere is so different now that you're in charge. It's—*

적으로나 그들이 좋은 파트너십을 유지해왔다는 사실만은 분명했다. 권은 공석이 된 지 오래인 N화장품 한국 지사장 자리를 노리고 있었다. 누구나 예측 가능한 인사(人事)였다. 그러나 한 달 전 뉴욕 본사는 와튼 MBA 출신의 코리언 아메리칸 브랜든을 한국에 파견했다. 권은 지나치게 분개했지만 그녀는 본사의 결정을 이해했다. 지방 대학 학사 장교 출신의 권은 애초에 브랜든의 상대가 될 수 없었다. 레스토랑 앞에는 브랜든의 은색 렉서스와 그녀의 소나타가 나란히 대기하고 있었다. 브랜든이 갑자기 제 차의 트렁크 쪽으로 다가갔다. 그가 꺼낸 것은 장미였다. 아이보리 빛 공단 리본으로 밑단을 묶은 붉은 장미가 한껏 만개해 있었다. 로맨틱한 밤이었다. 그 밤의 주연 여배우답게 그녀는 고른 치열을 자랑하며 활짝 웃었다.

토요일 오후 다섯 시

유리창 너머 흰 눈이 펑펑 무력하게 퍼붓고 있었다. 권은 전화를 받지 않았다. 자꾸 미끄러지는 손가락으로 권의 휴대폰 번호를 몇 번이나 누른 뒤에야 그녀는 오늘이 토요일임을 깨달았다. 주말이나 휴일에 개인 번호로 연락하지 않는 것은 첫 번째 철칙이었다. 재작년 어느 공휴일

well, it's much more lively. Brandon was looking right into her big-eye contact lenses.

While Brandon took care of the bill, she was in the women's room vomiting her meal. Keeping a size 26 waist was more aggravating and difficult than it looked, but she'd done it for 15 years now. She scrubbed her teeth, touched up her lipstick, and checked her cell phone for voice messages. There were three, all from Kwon. *You're with that asshole, aren't you?... I warned you, it's not going to work... I'll be waiting.* It was bad enough him being hypersensitive, but these days he was acting so juvenile. Not that she was ignorant of his feelings. Without his backing it would have taken her much longer to get to where she was in the company. For sure they had been a good team the last five years, both personally and professionally. The thing was, Kwon had been aiming for the directorship of the Korea branch of N Cosmetics, a position long vacant. And as far as anyone could tell, he was the heir apparent. But then a month ago, headquarters in New York City had dispatched Brandon, a Korean American with an MBA from the Wharton School of Finance, University of Pennsylvania. Kwon had flown into a rage, but she understood the decision.

에 있었던 아버지의 부음조차 권에게 바로 알리지 않았다. 좀 섭섭하더라. 직원들과 함께 뒤늦게 문상을 다녀간 권이 나중에 한마디 했지만 그녀는 짐짓 못 들은 척했다. 이럴 때 떠오르는 사람이 권뿐이라니. 그녀는 황황히 수화기를 내려놓았다. 그 아이가 왜, 어떻게, 그곳에 들어 있는 것일까. 뒤엉킨 실타래를 어디서부터 풀어야 할지 막막하기만 했다. 그녀는 엄지손톱을 잘근잘근 씹으면서 온 집 안을 서성였다. 누군가 소녀를 납치했다. 그리고 그녀의 차 트렁크에 유기했다. 그것 말고 다른 가설은 떠오르지 않는다. 불현듯 현기증이 인다. 소녀는 오늘, 회사에 출근하지 않았다. A4 용지가 똑 떨어졌잖아. 선미 안 나왔어? 암말 없이 빠지는 거 봐. 요즘 애들은 아무튼…… 이번 기회에 여상 나온 애로 아예 정직원을 하나 뽑았음 좋겠어요. 총무팀에서 들으라는 듯 윤이 큰 소리로 말했을 때조차 그녀는 어제 저녁 자신이 선미를 지하철 역까지 태워다주었다는 사실을 까맣게 잊고 있었다. 지하로 연결된 계단을 탁탁 뛰어 내려가던 소녀의 뒷모습. 그 조붓한 어깨와 합성섬유로 만든 코트, 검고 긴 머리 타래. 무릎에 스르르 힘이 빠졌다. N화장품 한국 지사의 직원 서른다섯 명 가운데 선미를 맨 마지막으로 본 사람은 바

Kwon, graduate of a provincial university thanks to an ROTC scholarship, couldn't hold a candle to Brandon.

The valets had Brandon's silver Lexus and her pearl-white Sonata ready and waiting. Brandon made for the trunk of his car and came back with a bouquet of roses. Red roses in full bloom, the bouquet held with a cream-colored satin bow. What a romantic evening. She was the queen of the night and her face blossomed in a smile, showing her perfect teeth.

Saturday, 5 p.m.

She gazed out the window at the relentless snowfall. Kwon wasn't answering at work. Only after several fumbling tries at punching in his number did she remember it was Saturday and everyone had left the office at noon. Rule number one: no calls to Kwon's cell phone on weekends and holidays. It was an ironclad rule: the year before last her father had passed away, and because it was a holiday, she had waited before informing Kwon. *I wish I'd known*, Kwon had said after paying his respects along with others from the office. She'd pretended she hadn't heard. *Kwon's the only one you can think*

로 그녀였다. 그녀는 그 자리에 주저앉았다. 크리스털 화병 속의 핏빛 장미 송이들이 그녀의 얼굴을 가만히 바라보았다.

그녀는 상당히 현실적인 사람이었다. 자유자재로 숟가락을 구부리며 초능력을 과시하는 마술사, 서울 하늘에 출몰한 유에프오의 사진 같은 것들은 믿어본 적이 없었다. 공권력이 증인의 사생활을 철저히 보호하는 장면은 할리우드 영화에나 나온다는 것도 잘 알고 있었다. 트렁크를 열었더니, 그 애가 들어 있었어요. 그 말을 입 밖에 내는 순간 자신에게 어떤 일이 벌어지리라는 것쯤은 충분히 예상할 수 있었다. 어젯밤 브랜든과 헤어진 뒤 권에게 들렀던 건 일종의 관성이었다. 권은 예상보다 더 많이 취해 있었고 막무가내로 그녀를 껴안으려 했다. 불가리 옴므 향과 구리텁텁한 입내가 뒤섞여 풍겨왔다. 모텔에 세 시간쯤 머물렀을까. 자정께 권은 카운터에 전화를 걸어 대리운전기사를 불러달라고 부탁했다. 권은 웬만해선 외박은 하지 않았고, 다음 날 아침에 둘 다 같은 옷을 입고 출근할 수는 없는 일이었다.

그녀는 밤 운전에 능숙했다. 분당까지는 이십 분이 좀 넘게 걸렸다. 지하 주차장에 주차를 하고 올라오면서 일

of at a time like this? she berated herself as she dropped the receiver. *How in God's name did she get in there?* She paced her studio, gnawing on her thumbnail, wondering how she would ever untangle herself from this mess. Someone had kidnapped the girl, then dumped her in the trunk—how else to explain it? A wave of dizziness swept over her. The girl hadn't shown up for work that morning. *We're out of paper*, she remembered Yun muttering to no one in particular. *Where's Seon-mi? She didn't call in sick or anything? Kids these days, they're useless...* And then in a loud enough voice for all the admin staff to hear: *From now on, why can't we get a girl full time, someone from a commercial high school.* She now realized she had forgotten dropping off the girl the previous evening. She visualized the girl disappearing down into the subway, heard the patter of her heels on the steps, saw her puny shoulders inside the coat with its synthetic weave, and the long dark clump of her ponytail. Her legs felt rubbery. Among the 35 employees of the Korea branch of N Cosmetics, she was the very last person to see Seon-mi alive. She plopped down onto the floor. The blood-red roses in the crystal vase silently regarded her.

층의 24시간 편의점에 들러 내일 신을 판탈롱 스타킹을 한 켤레 샀다. 낯익은 점원이 눈인사를 했다. 그러므로 그녀는 어젯밤, 세상을 납득시킬 만한 알리바이를 가지고 있지 않았다. 사흘 후면 신제품 발표 파티였다. 월요일 점심엔 인천공항으로 본사 수석 부사장을 마중 나가야 했다. 본사 최고위급 임원을 사박 오 일 동안 밀착 수행할 기회란 흔히 오는 것이 아니었다. 그녀는 최선을 다해 커리어를 쌓아왔다. 갈 길이 아직 멀었다. 판단은 순식간에 이루어졌다. 옷장에 걸린 겨울옷들은 대개 순모 백 퍼센트의 핸드 메이드 코트였다. 허리에서 끈을 묶거나 엉덩이를 살짝 가리거나 복사뼈까지 치렁치렁 늘어지는 색색의 코트들을 헤치고 모자 달린 솜 파카를 겨우 찾아냈다. 잠시 후, 이마 깊숙이 모자를 뒤집어쓰고 친친 목도리를 감은 여자가 엘리베이터 폐쇄회로 화면에 어렴풋하게 비쳤다. 흑백 모니터 속에서 그녀는 마치 검은 눈사람처럼 보였다.

토요일 오후 여덟 시 반

이민 가방은 이태원에서 샀다. 상점 주인은 접이식 가방을 삼단까지 펼치면 일 미터가 훌쩍 넘는 높이가 된다

Make no mistake, she was a practical person. She had never believed in magicians' tricks—the bending of a spoon with a twist of the fingers—or reports of UFOs in the skies over Seoul. And displays of government authority like witness protection programs? Only in Hollywood. *I popped the trunk and there she was.* Those words, the moment anyone heard them from her, would seal her fate. It was inertia that had led her to check in with Kwon after her dinner with Brandon. He was drunker than she'd expected, and when he grabbed her in a bear hug she was hit with a combination of foul breath and Bvlgari Homme cologne. How long had they been at the motel, three hours? It was around midnight when they'd checked out and Kwon had arranged for a designated driver to take him home. He rarely insisted on spending the night out—the two of them couldn't very well show up at work the next morning wearing the same clothes as on the previous day.

Driving at night didn't bother her, and she was back home in Bundang a little over 20 minutes after leaving the motel. She'd parked in the garage and on her way up had stopped at the convenience shop on the ground floor to buy a pair of knee-high

고 말했다. 중국산은 약해서 못 써요. 이놈은 얼마나 튼튼한지 어딜 들고 가도 끄떡없다니까. 무엇보다 어디서나 흔하게 볼 수 있는 디자인이 그녀를 안심시켰다. 함박눈은 서서히 잦아들고 새의 깃털 같은 눈발이 가붓가붓 흩날렸다. 도시는 어둠으로 뒤덮여 있었다. 자동차들은 기다시피 움직이는 중이었다. 도로변에 쌓인 눈의 양이 만만치 않았다. 잠수교를 건너 강남에 들어오면서부터 타이어가 여러 번 미끄러졌다. 그녀는 양손으로 핸들을 꼭 쥐고 정면만 뚫어져라 응시했다. 앞차 머플러에서 드라이아이스 같은 허연 김이 무럭무럭 뿜어져 나왔다.

권이 사는 아파트 단지는 서초동 대법원 앞에 있었다. 공중전화 부스 앞에 차를 댔다. 전화를 받은 건 변성기를 막 지낸 남자아이였다. 새 봄에 고등학생이 된다는 큰아들일 것이었다. 그녀는 권의 가족 사진을 본 적도, 보고 싶어한 적도 없었다. 여기는 회사입니다. 권 이사님 계신가요? 그녀는 빠르게 사무적으로 말하려고 애썼다. 아빠, 전화! 누구래? 몰라, 회사래. 수화기 너머의 대화가 꿈결처럼 들려왔다. 여보세요. 권의 저음이 가까이 들리자 이상스레 마음이 가라앉았다. 권은 십 분도 지나지 않아 허둥지둥 달려 나왔다. 꽤 놀란 눈치였다. 뒷자리에 실린 커

nylons for work in the morning. The usual clerk had nodded in recognition—so much for a credible alibi. The launch would be in three days. At lunchtime on Monday she had to go to Incheon Airport to pick up the Senior Executive Vice-President from headquarters. It wasn't often that anyone had the opportunity to escort someone at the very highest level from New York City, to have that person all to herself, and the VP would be staying four nights and five days. All these years she had done her best to build a career for herself, and she still had a long haul ahead of her. At that moment she made a decision. She rifled through the assortment of coats in her closet—most were hand-made, genuine wool, some of them with a strap around the waist, some of them half-coats, some of them maxis, an ensemble of colors—and finally she came across the hooded parka.

A short time later the fuzzy image of a woman appeared on the security cameras of the apartment complex. She was in the elevator, her features buried in a scarf and head covering. On the black-and-white screen she looked like a dark snowman.

다란 가방을 보자 그의 눈썹이 일그러졌다. 뭐야, 어디가? 적절한 답이 생각나지 않아서 그녀는 조용히 차를 출발시켰다. 타이어가 휘릭 헛바퀴를 돌았다.

짐작대로 권은 그녀의 얘기를 단숨에 알아듣지 못했다. 그녀는 다시 한 번 또박또박 설명했다. 이 차 트렁크에 사람이 들어 있어. 나도 좀 전에 알았어. 선미 알지? 회사의 아르바이트생, 바로 걔야. 권은 굉장히 얼떨떨한 표정을 지었다. 심지어 말을 더듬거리기까지 했다. 사, 사람이 들어 있다고? 지금 여기? 뒤, 뒤 트렁크 안에? 그래, 트렁크 안에. 권은 두툼한 손바닥으로 제 얼굴을 연신 문질러댔다. 그는 그녀의 예상보다 더 많이 당황하고 있는 듯했다. 입술을 달싹거리더니 겨우 한마디 했다. 주, 죽었다. 그녀는 솔직하게 대답했다. 모르겠어. 무서워서 그냥 뚜껑을 닫아버렸어. 자기가 좀 확인해줘. 순간 권의 낯빛이 변했다. 내, 내가? 그녀는 의미심장하게 고개를 끄덕였다. 응, 자기는 남자잖아. 분당까지 가는 동안 권은 손바닥으로 계속해서 얼굴을 비벼댔다. 이따금 한숨을 내쉬기도 했다. 눈은 그쳤지만 그녀는 조심스레 차를 몰았다. 분당으로 이어진 도시고속화도로에는 차량 통행이 거의 없었다. 몇 시간 지나 새벽이 되면 길은 끔찍한 빙판으로 변할 것

Saturday, 8:30 p.m.

In Itaewon she purchased a large travel bag on rollers, the so-called immigration bag. The merchant showed her how to unzip and expand it, to grow it over three feet from top to bottom. *This baby is invincible, you can take it anywhere. Steer clear of the Chinese ones—they're too flimsy.* Most important, you could see them everywhere, they wouldn't attract attention—and that's what reassured her. The snowfall had died down to a scattering of large feathery flakes. The city was blanketed with gloom. The traffic crawled along. A fair amount of snow had piled up along the sides of the road. She crossed the Jamsu Bridge to the south side of the river, where the driving got more slippery. She kept her focus dead ahead, hands clutching the wheel. Steam billowed from the tailpipe of the car in front of her, looking like dry ice.

Kwon lived in a complex in Seocho-dong, near the courthouse. She spotted a phone booth and pulled over. Kwon's son answered, the older one who would start high school in March, judging from the pubescent cracking of his voice. She'd never seen a photo of his family, nor did she want to. *Hello, this is N Cosmetics calling—is Director Kwon*

이다.

율동공원 주차장은 평소에도 밤이면 인적이 드문 곳이었다. 신도시의 건전한 시민들은 나이키 트레이닝복 차림으로 아침 조깅을 하고, 어린아이를 뒤에 태운 채 자전거를 타거나, 부근 음식점에서 점심을 먹고 식후 산책을 하는 용도로 근린공원을 이용했다. 차에서 내리기 전에 그녀는 권의 손에 라이터를 쥐어주었다. 주차장은 넓은 눈밭이었다. 권은 자동차 뒤로 미적미적 걸어갔다. 그의 운동화 발자국이 흰 눈 위에 선명히 찍혔다. 그가 트렁크 덮개를 여는 동안 그녀는 거무죽죽한 하늘을 올려다보았다. 세상에, 온몸이 뻣뻣해. 권은 몇 차례나 깊은 탄식을 뱉어냈다. 트렁크를 거세게 닫자마자 권은 왝왝 구역질을 했다. 바람이 찼다. 추위 때문이지 구토 때문인지 낯이 새파랗게 질려 있었다.

차 안이 훈훈했다. 권은 그녀가 건넨 휴지로 충혈된 눈자위와 입매를 꾹꾹 눌러 닦았다. 그가 안정을 되찾을 때까지 그녀는 잠자코 기다렸다. 그 정도의 인내심은 발휘할 수 있었다. 이윽고 그가 유리 조각을 삼킨 듯 갈라지는 음성으로 입을 열었다. 어쩌다 그랬어? 그녀는 제 귀를 의심했다. 무슨 소리야? 내가 그런 게 아니라니까. 권이 그

in? She spoke briskly, tried to sound business-like. *Dad, telephone!* And then Kwon's voice: *Who is it?* The son again: *Don't know—it's from work.* Like voices in a dream. And then Kwon came on, his voice muted. *Hello?* He sounded very close, and strangely enough, she began to relax. In less than 10 minutes he arrived, all in a flurry, obviously surprised. When he saw the huge travel bag in the back seat he grimaced. *What's that? Where are you going?* She couldn't think of a good answer, and pulled back onto the street, tires spinning.

As she'd expected, he didn't immediately comprehend her first attempt at an explanation; she had to repeat, slowly and precisely: *There's a body in the trunk. I just found it. It's Seon-mi. You know, Seon-mi, the office girl? It's her.* Kwon struggled to process the information. *A body? Now? Back there, in the trunk, the car trunk?* he faltered. *Yes, in the car trunk.* Kwon rubbed at his face with a fleshy palm. He was more flustered than she'd anticipated. His lips twitched. *She's d—dead?* She responded, *I don't know, I was so frightened I slammed the trunk shut.* Which was exactly what she had done. *Check for me, would you?* Instantly his color changed. *Who, me?* She gave him a determined nod. *Could*

녀의 가는 손목을 꽉 움커잡았다. 제발, 솔직하게 말해. 나한테는 그래도 되잖아. 가까이 들이댄 그의 입술에서 시척지근한 냄새가 진동했다. 그녀는 휙 손목을 뿌리쳤다. 도저히 이해가 안 돼, 도저히. 권이 제 머리통을 감싸 안고 중얼대는 모습을 보자 그를 부른 것에 대해 조금씩 후회가 일기 시작했다. 그러나 어쩔 도리가 없었다. 하다 못해 이민용 가방에 시체를 옮기거나, 땅을 파고 구덩이를 만드는 데도 남자의 힘이 필요했다. 그녀는 권의 어깨를 끌어안고 가만가만 다독였다. 괜찮아. 다 잘될 거야. 날 믿어.

일요일 오전 두 시

스무 살짜리 여자애의 실종은 지방 신문 단신 기사감도 못 되었다. 야트막한 야산은 어디에나 있었다. 사체를 야산에 암매장하는 것은 범죄 재연 방송에도 심심찮게 등장하는 보편적인 방법이었다. 먼저 이민용 가방에 소녀를 넣고 밤을 틈타 산에 오른다. 땅을 판 다음 가방에서 소녀를 꺼내 묻는다. 멀리 시 외곽으로, 강원도나 충청도까지 갈 수도 있었다. 실행에 옮길 만한 다른 방법들도 있었다. 팔당대교에서 46번 도로를 타고 조금만 달리면 남한강과

you? You're a man, you can do it. All the while, until they arrived in Bundang, he kept rubbing his face, and now and then heaved a sigh. The snow had stopped, but still she drove carefully. Not much traffic on the City Expressway. In a few hours the road surface would be a sheet of ice—she didn't want to think about it.

Yuldong Park saw little activity at night. Sound of mind, sound of body, the citizens of this new satellite city used their neighborhood park during the day, jogging first thing in the morning in their Nike training suits, going on a family bicycle ride, walking off their lunch at a nearby eatery. Before they got out, she handed Kwon a cigarette lighter just in case. The parking lot was a snowy expanse. Kwon trudged toward the back of the car, the soles of his sneakers leaving clear imprints in the snow. As he opened the trunk, she gazed at the murky sky. *Oh shit, she's all stiff.* He heaved one great sigh after another, then slammed the trunk shut and began retching. The wind was frigid, and whether from the cold or from his vomiting, his face turned white.

Back in the warm car, Kwon dabbed at his bloodshot eyes and cleaned his mouth with the tissue she handed him. She waited silently for him to settle

북한강이 합쳐지는 양수리가 나온다. 충주호나 청평호 같은 곳도 상관없을 것이다. 발목에 돌덩이를 묶거나 가방에 자갈을 넣어 가라앉히면 물체는 수면 위로 떠오르지 못한다. 최소한의 뒤탈도 남기고 싶지 않다면 불을 이용할 수도 있다. 열 손가락의 지문이나 아랫배의 맹장수술 자국, 선미가 선미임을 증거하는 그 어떤 흔적도 남지 않을 것이다. 노력한다면 방법은 얼마든지 있을 터였다.

그러나 권은 그녀의 계획을 제대로 들으려 하지 않았다. 술 없어? 그는 오피스텔에 들어오자마자 독주를 찾았다. 그녀는 규칙적인 생활인이었다. 찬장에 위스키를 감춰두고 홀짝이는 불면의 밤과는 거리가 멀었다. 권이 술을 사러 편의점에 내려간 동안 그녀는 전기 포트에 생수를 끓였다. 커피 생각이 간절했다. 새벽 두 시에 당도 높은 설탕이 뒤범벅된 일회용 커피 믹스를 타 마시다니, 스멀스멀 죄책감이 엄습했지만 하는 수 없었다. 살다 보면 어쩔 도리 없는 일이 생기고야 마는 것이다. 뜨겁고 들척지근한 액체가 목울대를 타고 깊숙이 흘러들어가자 거짓말처럼 잠깐 행복해졌다.

원룸으로 이루어진 오피스텔은 실평수만 스무 평에 가까웠다. 월넛 자재의 원목으로 마감된 실내에는 가스레인

down. She had patience to spare. When he spoke again his tone was glass-shard sharp: *How could you?* She couldn't believe what she was hearing. *What are you talking about—you think I did it?* Kwon grabbed her slender wrist and drew her close. *For God's sake tell me the truth, be honest with me.* She was hit with his fetid breath. She jerked her hand free. *I don't understand, I just don't get this.* At the sight of him muttering to himself, cupping the back of his head in his palms, she began to regret having called him. Well, too late now. Transferring the body to the immigration bag, digging a hole in the ground, burying it—she needed a man's help. She put an arm about him, patted him tenderly on the shoulder. *It'll be all right. It'll all work out. Trust me.*

Sunday, 2 a.m.

The disappearance of a twenty-year-old woman wouldn't rate a line even in the provincial dailies. And there were hills everywhere in the countryside, perfect for burying dead bodies, standard procedure in the crime shows on TV. First they would put her in the immigration bag, then they would take her up in the hills under cover of night. They would dig

지와 소형 냉장고, 원통형 세탁기 등의 기본 가전제품이 붙박이되어 있었다. 재작년 이곳으로 이사올 때 꼭 필요한 종류로만 가구를 새로 마련했다. 이태리제 싱글 침대는 헤드가 창가를 향하도록 배치해두었다. 맑은 날 잠자리에 들면 벌어진 커튼 틈으로 노르스름한 별이 올려다보였다. 카드 할부는 아직 좀 남아 있었지만 42인치 디지털 텔레비전과 DVD 플레이어 구입은 잘한 선택이었다. 「섹스 앤 더 시티」나 「앨리 맥빌」 같은 시트콤 시리즈를 빌려다 보고 천연 아로마향 젤로 샤워를 하면 휴일 저녁이 금방 지나고, 다시 한 주가 시작되곤 했다. 자신의 일상이 충분히 만족스러웠다는 걸 그녀는 새삼 깨닫고 있었다. 월요일 출근까지 서른 시간 남짓 남아 있었다. 그녀는 창밖의 암흑을 노려보았다.

권은 십 분도 안 되는 사이에 소주 한 병을 남김없이 비웠다. 알코올은 긴장을 이완시킬 뿐더러 현실을 잊게 만든다. 그는 제법 비장했다. 여기는 법치 국가야. 네 말이 정말로, 정말로 진실이라면 켕길 이유가 없어. 그녀는 코웃음이 나오는 대로 내버려두었다. 아랑곳없이 그는 두번째 소주병을 땄다. 친구 매형이 서울지검 부장검사야. 대학 후배 한 놈은 청와대에 있고. 네가 받을 데미지가 최

a hole, then take her out of the bag and bury her. They could go far outside the city, as far as Gangwon or Chungcheong. There were other options too. They could take the Paldang Bridge to route 46 and in a short distance reach Yangsu-ri, where the North Han and South Han rivers came together. Or they could dump the body and bag in a lake, say Chungju Lake or Chungpyung Lake, weighing it down beforehand with rocks tied to her ankles, or filling the bag with gravel, so it wouldn't float to the surface. And of course there was the ultimate leave-no-trace method—fire. Burning the body would be no fingerprints, no surgical scars, nothing to identify Seon-mi as Seon-mi. If they thought things through they could come up with any number of expedients.

The problem was, Kwon wasn't buying into her plan. *Anything to drink?* he asked as soon as they arrived at her officetel. By which he meant hard liquor. But her regimented lifestyle did not include keeping a bottle of whiskey for sipping away a sleepless night. While Kwon was downstairs at the convenience shop, she turned on the electric pot, itching for a cup of coffee. Here she was, resorting to a sugary instant-coffee packet at two in the morn-

소한이 되도록, 그 정도는 할 수 있어. 아무래도 그는 중요한 사실을 망각하고 있는 듯했다. 그녀는 그것을 상기시켜주었다. 이게 나 혼자만의 문제인 줄 알아? 그날 밤 내가 어디 있었는지 경찰이 그냥 넘어갈까?

권이 식탁 위에 유리잔을 탁 내려놓았다. 너 지금, 날 끌고 들어가겠다는 거야? 그녀는 싸늘한 시선으로 맞받아쳤다. 혐의를 벗는다 해도 소문이 퍼질 거야. 사람들이 얼마나 남 얘기를 좋아하는지, 이 바닥이 얼마나 좁은지 몰라서 그래? 처음부터 휘말려선 안 돼. 절대로! 권이 절레절레 고개를 흔들었다. 너 정말 무섭다, 하, 정말 무서워. 그는 반쯤 혀가 풀려 있었다. 그래서 요는, 지금 나한테 그걸 갖다 묻으라는 거 아냐, 미친놈처럼 언 땅에 삽질하라고? 그는 별안간 의자에서 벌떡 일어났다. 에이 쌍, 네가 저질러놓고 왜 나보고 뒤처리를 하라는 거야, 도대체 왜! 주거용 오피스텔은 벽이 얇았다. 그녀는 허겁지겁 권의 입을 막았다. 권이 우악스런 손아귀 힘으로 그녀의 손바닥을 떨쳐냈다. 나쁜 년, 처음부터 네가 죽인 거지? 그걸 모를 줄 알았어? 일요일 새벽 두 시. 이웃들이 깨어 있을지도 몰랐다. 그녀는 사력을 다해 권을 제지했다. 잔머리 좀 작작 굴려. 갈보 같은 년, 그동안 내 등골 파먹은 것

ing. A guilty feeling crept over her, but what could she do? If you lived long enough, situations came up that were out of your control. The hot, sweetish liquid coursed down deep inside her, and for a brief miraculous moment she felt almost happy.

Her 700-square-foot officetel studio was walnut-paneled and came with a gas stove, mini-fridge, front-loading washer-dryer, and other basic amenities. When she had moved in the year before last, she had brought only those furnishings that were absolutely necessary. Her Italian twin bed she had positioned with the headboard against the wall opposite the window. On a clear night she could lie in bed and look up between the curtains at the golden, starry heavens. And she liked her 42-inch digital television and the DVD player—a few more installments and they'd be paid off. *Sex and the City* and *Ally McBeal*—these and similar series she rented from a video outlet. Polish off an evening of visual entertainment with an herbal-gel shower and *poof,* another weekend was gone and a new work week awaited her. She couldn't complain about the life she led. A little more than 30 hours remained until she had to leave for work on Monday morning. She glared at the darkness beyond the window.

도 모자라서 이젠 이런 식으로 이용을 해? 그녀의 팔이 뒤로 꺾이고, 권의 눈동자가 희번덕댔다.

그녀는 저항했지만 속옷은 곧 벗겨졌다. 권은 양손으로 그녀의 어깨를 난폭하게 내리누르고 성기를 강제로 밀어 넣으려고 했다. 교접은 잘 되지 않았다. 그녀는 작은 소리도 내지 않고 모욕을 견뎠다. 그녀의 몸 위에서 몇 번인가 버둥대던 권은 기어이 질 안에 사정했다. 근 인생 최초의 강간이었다.

그녀는 마룻바닥에 고요히 누워 있었다. 권은 평상심을 회복한 듯했다. 주섬주섬 바지를 찾아 입고 혁대 버클을 채우는 권의 뒷모양을 그녀는 물끄러미 쳐다보았다. 권은 등을 보이며 냉장고 문 앞에 서 있었다. 그리고 담담하게 말했다. 이제, 경찰서에 가자. 그게 순서야. 그는 생수를 플라스틱 병째로 입술에 갖다 댔다. 그녀는 콧날을 찌푸렸다. 지난 오 년 동안 그런 지저분한 버릇을 눈치채지 못했다니 당혹스러웠다. 그녀는 천천히 권의 뒤로 다가갔다. 찬물을 벌컥벌컥 들이켜고 나서 권은 낮게 트림을 했다. 마지막 순간까지 그는 제 등 뒤로 다가선 그녀의 기척을 알아채지 못했다.

크리스털 꽃병은 여자 혼자 힘으로 들기에 꽤나 묵직했

In less than ten minutes Kwon had emptied his first bottle of *soju*. Relax and forget: she could see the alcohol working on him. *In case you forgot, we live by the rule of law in this country,* Kwon said, sounding like a tragic hero. *If what you say is true, if you're really telling the truth, then why get into a tizzy?* She dismissed the comments with a snort. Which he ignored as he cracked his second bottle of *soju. Listen—buddy of mine, his brother-in-law's a chief prosecutor for the city. Another one, a guy from college, is in the Blue House. I can work things so you get off light.* So much for the relaxing part. There remained a crucial fact he seemed to have forgotten, and she had to remind him: You're talking like this is only my problem. *Don't you think the police are going to be curious about where I spent last night?*

Kwon rapped his shot glass on the table. *What! You're going to drag me into this?* She countered with a frosty stare. *Even if you're cleared, the rumors will get around. People get off talking about other people. We live in a fishbowl, remember? I'm not going to let us get swept up in this—no way!* Kwon shook his head in disbelief. *You're scaring the shit out of me,* he huffed. *What a piece of work you are.*

다. 그녀는 그의 뒤통수를 있는 힘껏 후려쳤다. 남자는 이상하리만치 무기력하게 쓰러졌다.

바닥은 물과 피로 흥건했다. 산산조각 난 유리 파편들과, 꽃잎이 망가진 장미 송이들이 여기저기 흩뿌려져 있었다. 금요일 밤, 브랜든이 선물한 장미였다. 그동안 아주 긴 세월이 흐른 것 같기도 하고 눈 한 번 깜박인 것 같기도 했다. 허리를 구부리고 꽃 한 송이를 집어드는 순간 물레바늘처럼 날카로운 장미 가시가 검지 끝을 콕 찔렀다. 송골송글 핏방울 맺힌 손가락을 보자 오싹 소름이 끼쳤다. 그제야 모든 상황이 똑똑히 실감났다. 차에서 이민용 가방을 가져와 삼단으로 펼치고 축 늘어진 권의 시체를 질질 끌어다 담는 데까지 삼십 분도 안 걸렸다. 그가 체구가 크지 않은 남자인 게 다행스러웠다. 스스로의 손으로 하지 못할 일이란 세상에 아무것도 없었다. 가방의 지퍼를 잠그고 나서 그녀는 그것을 깨우쳤다.

청소를 마치자 급작스런 졸음이 밀려들었다. 그러나 메이크업을 지우지 않고 잠드는 건 피부 탄력에 치명타였다. 그녀는 늘 하던 대로 좌변기에 앉아 화장을 지웠다. 다이어트를 하는 여자들에게 만성 변비는 퍽 흔한 질환이었다. 그녀는 손바닥에 클렌징크림을 덜어 이마와 눈두

He was beginning to slur his words. *So—I get to bury what's in the trunk? You think I'm some stupid fuck who's going to dig a hole in the frozen ground, just for you?* He shot to his feet. *You expect* me *to clean up* your *mess? Fuck that.* She clapped a hand over his mouth—the officetel was designed as a residence but still the walls were thin. Kwon ripped the hand away. *Fucking bitch, you killed her, didn't you. You think I don't know that?* She struggled desperately to silence him—it was two in the morning but the neighbors might still be up. *You and your scheming little pea brain—you've been sucking the life out of me all along, you fucking whore, and now you want to use me for this?* He grabbed her arms, twisted them behind her back, glowered at her.

She resisted, but in no time he had her prone on the floor, panties down. Hands pressing down on her shoulders, he tried to penetrate her. She made no sound, determined to endure. She felt him thrash around and finally he entered her and ejaculated. It was the first time she had ever been raped.

She lay mute on the floor. Kwon seemed to have regained his senses. She watched as he gathered his pants, pulled them up, buckled them. He stood before the mini-fridge, still with his back to her.

덩, 뺨과 입술까지 가볍게 마사지한 뒤 화장솜으로 차근차근 닦아냈다. 환약 모양의 새까만 것들이 변기 물통 속으로 점점이 떨어졌다.

일요일 오전 열한 시 반

신도시 대형 교회의 주일 3부 예배는 가족 단위 신자들로 발 디딜 틈 없었다. 나 형제를 늘 위해 진실하고 날로 보는 자 늘 위해 정결코 담대하여 이 세상 환난중에 나 용감히 늘 승리하리라, 나 용감히 늘 승리하리라. 그녀는 제 두 손을 꽉 맞잡고 예절 바르게 찬송을 따라 불렀다.

월요일 오전 여섯 시

여느 때처럼 그녀는 여섯 시에 눈을 떴다. 지난밤 자정 뉴스에서 오늘 오후 경기 지역의 강수 확률이 70퍼센트라고 알려주었지만 우산을 준비하지는 않았다. 일기예보가 반드시 적중하는 것은 아니었기 때문이다. 출근길, 이웃들과 우연히 마주쳤다면 다들 그녀가 멀고 긴 여행을 떠난다고 추측했을 테지만 엘리베이터에서 내려 지하 주차장을 떠날 때까지 아무와도 부닥치지 않았다. 가방이 엄청나게 무거웠지만 타인의 도움은 기대하지 않았다. 이면

Come on, he said. *We're going to the police. Should have gone there in the first place.* His voice was serene. He drank water from the two-liter plastic bottle, not bothering with a glass. She frowned. Five years she'd known him and she hadn't been aware of that disgusting habit? She rose and approached him, slowly and quietly. She heard him gulp the water, heard a muffled burp. He never heard her coming. A crystal vase might be too heavy for some women, but she managed to heft it, then brought it down with all her strength against the back of his skull. Surprise—he went down like a rag doll.

On the floor a pool of blood and water. Chunks and shards of glass, crushed rose blossoms—Brandon's gift from Friday evening—scattered about. It felt like so much time had passed; then again, it felt like the blink of an eye. She bent over to retrieve one of the rose sprigs and a thorn, sharp as Sleeping Beauty's needle, pricked her index finger. A bead of blood formed; she shuddered. And everything came back to her. She brought the immigration bag in from the car, grew it out to full volume, dragged and stuffed Kwon's slack form inside—thank heaven he wasn't a big bruiser of a man—and zipped the bag shut. The entire process

도로는 눈이 녹아 질척하고 지저분했다. 평소보다 약간 늦은 출발이었다. 도시고속화도로는 뻥 뚫려 있었다. 트렁크는 다만 고요했다. 겨울 해가 운전석 위로 비스듬히 쏟아지자 갑자기 좀 외롭다는 생각이 들었다. 어딘가, 빛이 들어오지 않는 작고 캄캄한 공간에서 사지를 웅크리고 잠들고 싶었다. 아기집 같은 동굴 속! 비로소 그녀는 모든 비밀을 이해할 것도 같았다. 그날, 어쩌면 선미도 그녀와 같은 기분이었을 것이다. 안온하고 조용한 곳을 찾다가 제 손으로 트렁크 덮개를 열고 들어가, 그 안에서 곤한 잠을 청했을 것이다. 그렇게 생각하자 왠지 마음이 푸근해졌다.

열 시에는 런칭 행사 실무자들끼리의 미팅을 주재했다. 파티 참석을 약속한 연예인들 숫자가 꽤 많다고 했다. 굿뉴스였다. 회의를 마치고 자리에 돌아오는데 최 대리가 그녀의 옷소매를 잡아끌며 속살거렸다. 차장님, 이거 비밀인데요. 권 이사랑 선미, 글쎄 그 둘 사이가 심상치 않았대요. 나 참, 회사 땡땡이치고 지금도 같이 있는 거 아닌지 몰라. 그녀는 흥미롭게 눈망울을 반짝였으나 시간 관계상 더 심도 깊은 대화를 나누지는 못했다. 브랜든이 기다리고 있었다. 이제부터 그녀와 브랜든은 본사의 수석

took less than thirty minutes. There came a realization—was there anything on this earth that she couldn't do with her own two hands?

She finished the clean-up and was hit by a wave of drowsiness. But if she fell asleep as she was, her skin would never forgive her. So as she always did, she settled herself on the pot and began to remove her makeup. Constipation was a constant complaint for women who watched their weight, and as she worked the cleansing cream into her forehead and eyelids, her cheeks and lips, then wiped with a cotton pad, she heard from the toilet boil the plink and plop of her small, dark stools, which reminded her of pellets of Chinese medicine.

Sunday, 11:30 a.m.

The mega-church she attended in this new satellite city offered three services on the day of our Lord, and all three were packed with families. *I would be true, for there are those who trust me. I would be pure, for there are those who care. I would be strong, for there is much to suffer. I would be brave, for there is much to dare. I would be brave, for there is much to dare.* She sang with the congregation,

부사장을 공항으로 영접 나가야 했다. 매끈한 서류 가방을 들고 사무실을 나서는 그녀의 뒷모습은 우아하고 완벽했다.

은색 렉서스의 옆자리에 올라타면서 그녀는 저 멀리 세워진 자신의 자동차에 흘깃 시선을 주었다. 차에는 아무런 문제도 없어 보였다. 2002년형 EF 소나타. 사 년 연속 부동의 베스트셀러 1위. 대한민국 도로 어디에서나 흔히 볼 수 있는 모델이었다. 이제 겨우 천 킬로미터를 주행했을 뿐이다. 아직 갈 길이 멀었다. 그녀는 자신의 새 차가 아주 마음에 들었다.

『낭만적 사랑과 사회』, 문학과지성사, 2011(2003)

hands clasped together, a proper parishioner.

Monday, 6 a.m.

As usual she woke up at six to the alarm clock. The weather forecast on the late-night news had mentioned a 70 percent chance of precipitation today in the Seoul-Gyeonggi region, but she didn't bother with an umbrella. The weather forecast wasn't always accurate. If she were to encounter any of the other residents, they would assume she was leaving on a long trip to distant parts, but in the event, she arrived at her car without seeing a soul. The immigration bag was ponderous, but she didn't anticipate needing assistance from anyone. The streets were a slushy mess. She was starting out a few minutes later than usual, but the City Expressway was wide open. All was quiet in the trunk. The sun had just come up and as its rays slanted through the driver-side window, she felt an urge to curl up in some dark, cramped space where no light would enter, a womblike chamber—it was such a lonely feeling! Seon-mi must have felt the same way, must have thought she'd discovered a quiet and comfy place, must have opened the trunk and climbed inside, seeking a deep, sound sleep.

She was somehow comforted by this thought.

At 10 a.m. the launch team met. A number of celebrities and personalities would be in attendance, one of them reported. *Sounds good*, she said. Back at her desk she was approached by Choe, who tugged gently at her sleeve before whispering, *Just between you and me, Mr. Kwon and Seon-mi seem to be getting it on. Can you believe it? And guess who's playing hookey today?* She pretended to be intrigued, but a person working under time constraints can't afford lengthy conversations. Brandon was waiting. They had to leave shortly for the airport to welcome the Senior Executive Vice-President flying in from New York City. Spiffy briefcase in hand, she was elegance itself as she left the office.

From inside the silver Lexus she spotted her pearl-white Sonata off in the distance. It looked so innocent and trouble-free. A 2002 Hyundai Sonata EF. Top-selling make the last four years, and a familiar sight on the highways and byways of the Republic of Korea. She'd only racked up a thousand kilometers on it and she still had a long haul ahead of her. Her new car suited her just fine.

Translated by Bruce and Ju-chan Fulton

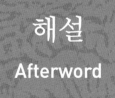

해설

Afterword

'낭만적 사랑'과 전략적 사랑

차성연(문학평론가)

   '낭만적 사랑'을 일종의 신화라 말할 수 있는 이유는 모두가 선망하지만 아무나 이룰 수 없는 허상이라는 의미가 포함되어 있기 때문이다. 그럼에도 불구하고, 어느 날 운명과도 같은 연인을 만나서 '자율적으로' 사랑을 나누고 '자발적인 선택'을 통해 결혼하여 자식을 낳고 가족을 이루어 평생을 함께 하는 '낭만적 사랑'의 형식을 아직도 많은 이들이 선망하는 것도 사실이다. '낭만적 사랑'이 결혼과 가족 제도를 통해 현재의 체제를 그대로 유지하려는 지배 이데올로기임은 명백하지만 거기에는 사회가 인정하는 제도적 범주 내에서 개인의 성적·사회적 욕망을 적당히 처리하고자 하는 개개인의 자발적 승인이 포함되어

"Romantic Love" and Strategic Love

Cha Seong-yeon (literary critic)

"Romantic love" is a myth because it embodies the connotation of illusion as something everyone covets but only few attain. Nevertheless, people still fantasize about living out this formula of "romantic love"—a fateful romantic encounter, "free-willed" love, marriage and childrearing as a "voluntary act," and a lifetime together. While there is no doubt this notion of "romantic love" is part of the prevailing ideology to maintain the current status quo through marriage and the family system, but it also include the individual desire to more or less satisfy individual sexual, social desires within the socially acceptable arena. Then again, the notion of the "free-

있다. 또한 이 모두는 '자율적 개인'의 '자발적 선택'이라는 또 하나의 신화에 의해 지탱되고 있다.

정이현의 「트렁크」에는 사회적으로 성공한 커리어 우먼이 되기 위해 자신의 일상을 철저하게 조정, 배치하고 그에 맞추어 자신의 역할을 연기하는 여성이 등장한다. 그녀의 일상은 오직 성공한 커리어 우먼이라는 목표를 향해 "군더더기 없이 심플하게" "촘촘히 조직되어" 있다. 그녀의 차에 아기자기한 장식이나 불필요한 짐이 없는 것처럼. 하지만 그녀가 얼마 전에 바꾼 2002년형 진주색 EF 소나타 골드의 트렁크 안에는 시체가 된 한 소녀가 웅크리고 있다. 그녀의 매끄러운 연기와 꽉 짜인 일상을 위험에 빠뜨리는 트렁크의 시체, 그럼에도 불구하고 소녀의 시체와 더불어 한 구의 시체를 더해 트렁크에 가두고 아슬아슬한 연기를 계속해 나가는 여성이 「트렁크」의 주인공이다.

「트렁크」의 '그녀'는 '낭만적 사랑'의 허구성을 간파하고 있다. 그녀는 "토익이나 워드 자격증이 아니라 쌍꺼풀 때문에 직장을 얻게 되리라고는 짐작도 못"한 성형외과 병원을 첫 직장으로 하여 몇몇 곳을 전전하다 지금의 N화장품 한국 지사 차장 자리에까지 오르게 되었다. 이러한

willed" individual and "voluntary act" are also myths.

Jeong Yi-hyun "In the Trunk" portrays a woman who maintains strict control over her life, keeps everything in perfect order, and acts out her role flawlessly in order to become a successful career woman. Her daily routine is "simple, uncluttered," and "fastidiously woven" to achieve her goal of success. Even in her new 2002 Pearl EF Sonata Gold, cutesy decorations are nowhere to be found. However, there is a corpse of a dead girl curled up in the trunk of her car. In spite of the body that may put her seamless acting and tight schedule in jeopardy, the protagonist adds another body to her In the trunk and continues her walk along the tightrope that is her life.

The protagonist of "In the Trunk" is thoroughly aware of the fictitiousness of "romantic love." Her first job, receptionist at a plastic surgeon's office, is obtained "not through a good TOEIC score or a Word Processor license, but her double eyelids." She climbs the corporate ladder as she changes jobs and makes it to deputy head of a department at N Cosmetics. Through her experience, she learns early on that there is only a small class of people who

경험을 토대로 그녀는 '낭만적 사랑'을 피상적으로나마 누릴 수 있는 계층이 이 사회에서 얼마나 제한적인지를 일찌감치 깨달았을 터이다. '낭만적 사랑'은 부유한 집안에서 태어나 안정적인 직장과 미래를 가진 이들에게만 허용되는 것이기에, 정이현의 인물들은 그러한 상류층에 소속되기 위해 '낭만적 사랑'이라는 신화를 역이용한다. 고속 승진을 위해 권 이사와 불륜 관계를 유지하거나 '권'이 노리고 있는 한국 이사장직에 새로 부임한 브랜든과 연인 사이가 되는 등, '그녀'는 커리어 우먼으로서의 성공을 위해 자신의 성적 매력을 가꾸고 활용하며 그들이 원하는 역할을 매끄럽게 수행한다. 그녀에게 '사랑'은 목표를 위한 하나의 전략이며 언제나 군림하기만 했던 남성들은 그녀의 전략에 이용당하는 존재가 된다. 그녀와 불륜 관계에 있는 '권'은 브랜든이 부임하자 그녀에게 버림받고 급기야 "하다못해 이민용 가방에 시체를 옮기거나, 땅을 파고 구덩이를 만드는 데도 남자의 힘이 필요"하다는 이유로 '그녀'에게 불려 나온다. 하지만 '권'이 순순히 받아들이지 않자 '그녀'는 권을 살해하고 손수 이민용 가방에 시체를 넣은 뒤 "스스로의 손으로 하지 못할 일이란 세상에 아무것도 없었다."고 깨우친다.

can afford romantic love, however superficially. Since "romantic love" is only granted to those who are born into money and are guaranteed a stable job and future, Jeong Yi-hyun characters abuse the "romantic love" myth to make their way into high society. She keeps up with her affair with Kwon, a member of the board of directors, to ensure her speedy promotion, becomes lovers with Brandon, the new head of the board of directors whose job Kwon is going after, and carries out the roles that they want her to play by cultivating and utilizing her sexual charm to its full potential—all for the sake of her own success. For her, love is a strategy that allows her to win the power game with men who used to have the upper hand but have now become her pawns. She abandons Kwon for Brandon when Kwon does not make the head of the board of directors, but is later summoned by her because "you need the muscles of a man to put a body in a suitcase and dig a ditch." But when Kwon is not as compliant as she had hoped, she kills him, puts the body in the suitcase herself, and realizes that "there's nothing in the world I can't handle by myself."

But was her strategy indeed a success? Even after

하지만 과연 '그녀'의 전략은 성공적인 것일까? 시체를 처리하고도 "늘 하던 대로 좌변기에 앉아 화장을 지우고" 살인을 저지르고도 주일 예배에 버젓이 참석하는, 표면적으로 철저해 보이는 그녀의 연기와 전략은, 트렁크에 들어 있는 시체가 증명하듯 사실 많은 부분을 숨기고 외면함으로써 그렇게 보일 뿐이다. "차장님, 이거 비밀인데요. 권 이사랑 선미, 글쎄 그 둘 사이가 심상치 않았대요."라는 진술이 암시하고 있는 소녀(선미)에 대한 '그녀'의 질투, 그로 인한 살해 가능성. 그리고 "어딘가, 빛이 들어오지 않는 작고 캄캄한 공간에서 사지를 웅크리고 잠들고 싶었다. 아기집 같은 동굴 속! 비로소 그녀는 모든 비밀을 이해할 것도 같았다. 그날, 어쩌면 선미도 그녀와 같은 기분이었을 것이다. 안온하고 조용한 곳을 찾다가 제 손으로 트렁크 덮개를 열고 들어가, 그 안에서 곤한 잠을 청했을 것이다."라는 진술에서 유추할 수 있는 그녀의 실존적 고독, 스스로 선택한 전략으로부터 자기 자신 역시 훼손되고 있다는 자각, 이 모든 것으로부터 벗어나 자궁과도 같은 공간으로 돌아가고픈 회귀 욕망. 이렇게 보면 '낭만적 사랑'의 허구성을 간파했던 '그녀' 역시 그것을 전략적으로 이용하고자 했으나 사회적 성공과 생존이라는 더 절

disposing of the body, she "sits on the toilet and removes her makeup," and coolly attends Sunday service after killing someone. Her acting and strategy seems perfect on the outside, but it only appears so because she is hiding and avoiding a great deal of problems underneath, as evidenced by the corpse in the trunk. "You didn't hear this from me, but Kwon and Seon-mi—there's something going on between the two." This tip from a co-worker suggests the protagonist may have been jealous of Seon-mi (the girl in the trunk), and perhaps killed her. Also, her existential solitude, the realization that her own strategy will be her ruin, and the desire to escape from it all and return to a womb-like place is gleaned from her thoughts, "She wanted to curl up and sleep in a small, dark space where the light cannot get to her. A cave like a baby's pouch! She felt she could finally understand everything. Seon-mi must have felt the same way. She was searching for a peaceful, quiet place when she saw the trunk and climbed in on her own accord. She took a much needed nap." This illustrates that in spite of her understanding of the fictitious nature of "romantic love" and her effort to use it as a strategy, the greater ideological forces of social success and sur-

대적인 이데올로기에 포획되어 소모되고 있었음을 알 수 있다. 그녀에게 커리어우먼으로서의 성공이란 철저하게 혼자인 사회에서 자기 정체성을 확인할 수 있는 유일한 방법인 동시에 물질적 조건을 획득하기 위한 생존 전략이기 때문이다.

1990년대 문학의 여성들이, 남성 중심적 '낭만적 사랑'의 구도 내에서 주어지는 파트너로서의 역할에 문제를 제기하며 스스로 주체가 되어 파트너를 선택하려는 양상을 보여 왔다면, 정이현 소설의 여성들은 필요에 따라 기꺼이 남성이 원하는 파트너로서의 역할을 연기함으로써 자신이 원하는 것을 얻고자 한다. 「트렁크」가 발표된 2003년의 한국 사회는 IMF 금융 위기를 거치고 '생존'이 절체절명의 가치로 부상하기 시작하던 시기이다. 이즈음부터 개인이 자유롭게 선택할 수 있는 것이란 이 사회에서 지극히 제한되어 있으며 '사랑'과 같은 감정의 영역 역시 마찬가지임이 공공연해졌다. 정이현의 소설에 그려진 사랑은 선택 가능한 '낭만적 사랑'에서 생존을 위한 전략적 수단으로서의 사랑으로 이행해 가는 경계를 보여준다.

vival always had a firm grip on her. To her, success as a career woman was the only way for her to establish her identity in a society where people are completely alone, and also a survival strategy to obtain material wealth.

Whereas women writers in the 1990s problematized the role of the partner in the male-centered structure of "romantic love," and argued for the right to choose their own partners, Jeong Yi-hyun female characters seek what they want by gladly acting out the male fantasy. In 2003, when "In the Trunk" was published, Korea was just getting over a fatal financial crisis and its people prized survival above all else. It was common knowledge at the time that there were very few things over which the individual had control, and this included love and the emotional sphere. Love in Jeong Yi-hyun stories show us the crossover of "romantic love" as a choice to "strategic love" as a survival tactic.

비평의 목소리

Critical Acclaim

정이현의 여성 인물들은 남성들의 공포와 욕망의 대상화된 표상이 아니라, 한 여성 작가에 의해 전략적으로 구성된 여성 캐릭터이다. 이 캐릭터는 좀 더 의식적인 차원에서 로맨스, 결혼, 가족, 국가 등을 둘러싼 제도적 이데올로기에 균열을 만드는 존재이다. 중요한 것은 대중문화 속의 악녀들이 '남성적인 시선'의 구성물인 경우라면, 정이현 소설의 인물들은 여성 자신의 욕망이 빚어낸 캐릭터들이라는 점, 영화 속의 악녀들은 자신의 '시선'과 '언어'를 갖지 못하고 남근적 카메라에 의해 대상화되지만, 정이현 소설 속의 그녀들은 자신의 시선으로 세계를 해석하고 자신의 언어로 말하려 한다.

The female characters of Jeong Yi-hyun are not are not objects conjured up by male fantasy, but characterizations of women strategically planned by a woman writer. These characters dismantle on a more conscious level the ideologies that govern romance, marriage, family, and nation. Whereas the women portrayed as she-devils in popular culture are products of the male perspective, Jeong Yi-hyun characters are products of women's own desires. While the she-devils in film are devoid of their own language and perspective, and objectified by the phallocentric lens, Jeong Yi-hyun characters interpret the world through their own perspectives and

정이현의 소설들은 여성적 위장술과 그 위장의 무기로서의 자기 언술을 통해, 여성들의 내밀한 욕망을 드러낸다.

이광호

그동안 한국의 여성 소설은 여성적 문법의 개발과 남성적 억압 구조의 의식화라는 문학적 성취를 쌓아왔으며, 특히 1990년대 여성 문학은 여성적 내면의 탐구와 가부장적 가족 제도로부터의 탈출의 욕망을 보다 적극적으로 드리냈다. 여성의 존재 탐색 내면에 근거한 고백의 화법과 가족 및 결혼으로부터의 일탈을 의식화하는 불륜의 서사가 그것이다. 정이현의 소설들이 특징적인 것은, 내면과 불륜 모두에 대해서 전략적인 거리를 두고 있다는 점이다. 그의 소설에서 내면은 민얼굴 드러내기가 아니라 화장하기의 방식으로 제시되며, 불륜은 진정한 여성적 자아를 발견하는 위험한 여행이 아니라 비밀을 만드는 즐거운 작업으로 바뀌어 나타난다.

김동식

대중 소비문화와 진정한 고급문화 사이에서, 대중소설이나 홈드라마와 문제적 소설 문법 사이에서 위태로운 경

put things in their own words.

Jeong's stories illuminate the furtive desires of women through her characters' feminine camouflage and their own language, which is the tool of their camouflage.

Lee Gwang-ho

Korean fiction by women writers has made the literary accomplishment of unearthing the female voice and developing consciousness of the oppressive patriarchal system. Especially in the 1990s, women's literature exhibited a much more active desire for women's self-examination and escape from the patriarchal family structure, the result of which were confessional narratives based on women's explorations of the inner self, and the manifestation of the escape fantasy from family and marriage that was the narrative of extramarital affairs. Jeong Yi-hyun stories stand out because her characters always keep a strategic distance, whether it is their inner self or an extramarital affair. The inner self is expressed not through a woman's unadorned face, but how she conceals her face, and the extramarital affair is not a perilous journey to finding herself, but a fun project of mak-

계선의 줄타기를 하면서 기존의 연애, 이성애, 결혼, 양성 불평등, 일상성, 몸의 문제 등 여러 제도적 현상적 문제들에 탈을 내고 구멍을 내어 새로운 감각의 진실을 찾아 나선 것도 중요하지만, 그 심층에서 약동하는 정치적 무의식이 좀 더 중요하다. 자기 위안의 포즈에 젖어들 수밖에 없는 소비사회, 접속 시대의 인간군상 일반이 지니고 있는 불안의 무의식이 그것이다. 불안하기에 접속한다. 그 것이 더 큰 불안의 둥지일지라도 접속하고 본다. 이런 접속이 계속되면 될수록, 수많은 접속의 네트워크 속에서 실제로는 자기 안에 갇힌 허구적 존재가 되기 십상이다. 이 속절없는 허구성을 정이현은 정치적 무의식의 그물로 길어 올린다.

우찬제

싸스비(Jacqueline Sarsby)의 사회적 통찰을 문학적으로 빌려온 듯이 보이는 정이현의 소설집 『낭만적 사랑과 사회』는 낭만적 사랑이 결혼으로 귀결되는 과정을 여성의 눈으로 바라보고 있다. 물질적 욕망을 적극적으로 표출하는 여성상의 등장은 한국 소설의 새로운 면모라 할 만하다. 정이현 소설의 여성들은 낭만적 사랑을 덧씌우는 사

ing a secret.

Kim Dong-sik

It is important to walk a tight rope between popular culture and high culture proper, between the melodramatic and the problematic, to break apart preexisting systemic, phenomenological issues such as relationships, heterosexuality, marriage, gender inequality, the Heideggerian timefulness, and the body in search of new truths, but the political subconscious palpitating beneath the surface of the phenomena. Consumerist society putting on airs of self-pity or the subconscious anxiety shared among the general populace in an age of connection are examples of such phenomena. Even when people know that they are about to access a greater crucible of anxiety, they connect nonetheless. These connections culminate in a network where the individual is ironically turned into a spurious entity trapped within herself. Jeong pulls up this hollow fictitiousness with a net of political subconscious.

U Chan-je

A short story collection that reads like a literary

회의 편견과 관습에서 자유롭다. 사랑이 연출될 수 있음을 과시하는 여성들의 출현은 이전의 소설에서는 보기 드문 것이었다. 여성 인물들은 자신의 소비 욕망을 당당히 드러냄으로써 가부장제의 물신화된 사회가 여성의 육체와 정신에 씌운 허위의식을 가차 없이 뒤집는다. 소비사회의 여성적 욕망을 충실하게 따른다는 점에서 정이현 소설의 인물들은 현대적인 의미를 지닌다고 할 수 있다.

백지연

implementation of Jacqueline Sarsby's insight into society, *Romantic Love and Society* follows the progress of romantic love to marriage from a woman's perspective. Literary heroines who do not shy away from expressing their materialistic needs has been a rarity in Korean literature until Jeong Yi-hyun, who writes characters who are free from the social customs and prejudices that try to disguise things under the blanket of "romantic love." Few female characters in Korean literature were as forward about their staged romance as Jeong's characters. Unashamed to express their consumeristic desires, these female characters subvert the fetishization imposed on women's bodies and mind by a patriarchal society.

Baek Ji-yeon

정이현

1972년 서울에서 태어난 정이현은 2002년 단편 「낭만적 사랑과 사회」로 제1회 《문학과 사회》 신인문학상을 받으면서 작가 생활을 시작했다. 성신여대 정치외교학과와 여성학과 대학원을 나왔고 서울예술대학교 문예창작과를 졸업했다. 자전소설로 알려져 있는 단편 「삼풍백화점」을 참고하면, 학창 시절을 강남 지역에서 보냈으며 전형적인 서울 중산층의 삶을 살았던 것으로 추측할 수 있다. 정이현 소설의 특징이라 할 만한 소비문화에 대한 세부적인 묘사와 구체적인 감각은 이러한 환경에서 영향을 받은 것으로 보인다. 한국 대중문화가 부흥기를 맞았던 1990년대 초반에 감수성이 예민한 청년 시절을 보내면서 대중문화적 감성이 자연스럽게 몸에 배었을 것이고, 1994년 성수대교 붕괴, 1995년 삼풍백화점 붕괴 사고 등을 생생한 현장으로 목격하며 오로지 앞을 향해 달려가던 한국형 성장의 이면을 목도했을 것이다. 물질적·문화적 풍요로움 이면의 내면적 고독과, 정치 사회적 역학 관계와 연루된 치졸한 욕망의 싸움을 꿰뚫어보는 작가 특유의 날카로운 시

Jeong Yi-hyun

Born in Seoul, 1972, Jeong Yi-hyun made her debut as a writer with "Romantic Love and Society" in 2002 through the *Literature and Society* New Writer Award. She holds an undergraduate degree in politics and foreign diplomacy, and a graduate degree in women's studies from Sungshin Women's University, and studied creative writing at Seoul Institute of the Arts. According to her autobiographical story, "Sampoong Department Store," she spent her teens in Gangnam as a typical middle-class Seoul resident. Jeong characteristically detailed descriptions of consumer culture and true-to-life sensibility may be attributed to her environment. Spending her impressionable youth in the early 1990s when popular culture flourished in Korea, her sensitivity to popular culture would have become second nature to her, and witnessing the 1994 Seongsu Bridge collapse and the 1995 Sampoong Department Store collapse would have been a testament to the flipside of the "Korean economic model" that raced ahead fasted than it could afford

선은 정이현 작품세계의 기반이 되었다.

2003년 첫 소설집 『낭만적 사랑과 사회』를 출간하여 도발적인 새로운 여성 작가의 출현을 알렸다. 1990년대 문학의 주류였던 여성 문학이 내면으로의 침잠이나 불륜을 통한 자기 확인의 서사를 보여주었던 것과는 확연히 다른 지점을 보여주었다는 점에서 문제적인 작품집으로 평가되었다. 신문 연재를 거쳐 2006년 출간된 『달콤한 나의 도시』는 큰 반향을 일으켜 2008년 TV 드라마로 각색, 방영되기도 했다. 한국형 직릿(Chick lit)소설로 일컬어지는 『달콤한 나의 도시』는, 미혼 여성의 일과 사랑을 도회적 감수성과 도발적이고 감각적인 문체로 그려냄으로써 대중적인 호응을 얻었다. 2007년 두 번째 작품집 『오늘의 거짓말』, 2011년 장편 『너는 모른다』를 출간하였으며, 알랭 드 보통과 2년여의 공동 작업 끝에 2012년 장편 『사랑의 기초』를 펴냈다. 「타인의 고독」으로 제5회 이효석문학상(2004년)을, 「삼풍백화점」으로 제51회 현대문학상(2006년)을, 같은 해 2006년 오늘의 젊은 예술가상을 받았다.

to. Her shrewd insight that turns our attention to the inner loneliness behind the material, cultural prosperity, and the spiteful fight of desire enmeshed with political and social dynamics became the building blocks of Jeong writing.

The publication of Jeong short story collection, *Romantic Love and Society* signaled the appearance of a provocative new woman writer. The book was recognized as seminal work in that it a represented a viewpoint completely different from the 1990s women writers' narrative of self-affirmation through withdrawal or extramarital affairs. *My Sweet City*, first a newspaper serial that was later published in 2006, was enthusiastically received and adapted for television in 2008. *My Sweet City*, known as the prototypical Korean "chick lit," won popular acclaim by portraying the career and romance of single women through an urban sensibility and provocative, sensual narrative style. Her second short story collection, *Today's Lie*, was published in 2007, and published *You Don't Know*, a novel, in 2011. In 2012, she published *Basics of Love* through a two-year collaboration with Alain de Botton. She received the Yi Hyoseok Literary Prize for "Another's Solitude" in 2004, the Hyeondae Literary Prize for "Sampoong

Department Store" in 2006, and Today's Young
Artist Award in the same year.

번역 **브루스 풀턴, 주찬 풀턴**
Translated by Bruce Fulton and Ju-chan Fulton

브루스 풀턴, 주찬 풀턴은 함께 한국문학 작품을 다수 영역해서 영미권에 소개하고 있다. 『별사-한국 여성 소설가 단편집』 『여행자-한국 여성의 새로운 글쓰기』 『유형의 땅』(공역, Marshall R. Pihl), 최윤의 소설집 『저기 소리 없이 한 점 꽃잎이 지고』, 황순원의 소설집 『잃어버린 사람들』 『촛농 날개-악타 코리아나 한국 단편 선집』 외 다수의 작품을 번역하였다. 브루스 풀턴은 서울대학교 국어국문학과에서 박사 학위를 받고 캐나다의 브리티시컬럼비아 대학 민영빈 한국문학 및 문학 번역 교수로 재직하고 있다. 다수의 번역문학기금과 번역문학상 등을 수상한 바 있다.

Bruce and Ju-chan Fulton are the translators of several volumes of modern Korean fiction, including the award-winning women's anthologies Words of Farewell: Stories by Korean Women Writers (Seal Press, 1989) and Wayfarer: New Writing by Korean Women (Women in Translation, 1997), and with Marshall R. Pihl, Land of Exile: Contemporary Korean Fiction, rev. and exp. ed. (M.E. Sharpe, 2007). Their most recent translations are the 2009 Daesan Foundation Translation Award-winning There a Petal Silently Falls: Three Stories by Ch'oe Yun (Columbia University Press, 2008); The Red Room: Stories of Trauma in Contemporary Korea (University of Hawai'i Press, 2009), and Lost Souls: Stories by Hwang Sunwŏn (Columbia University Press, 2009). Bruce Fulton is co-translator (with Kim Chong-un) of A Ready-Made Life: Early Masters of Modern Korean Fiction (University of Hawai'i Press, 1998), co-editor (with Kwon Young-min) of Modern Korean Fiction: An Anthology (Columbia University Press, 2005), and editor of Waxen Wings: The Acta Koreana Anthology of Short Fiction From Korea (Koryo Press, 2011). The Fultons have received several awards and fellowships for their translations, including a National Endowment for the Arts Translation Fellowship, the first ever given for a translation from the Korean, and a residency at the Banff International Literary Translation Centre, the first ever awarded for translators from any Asian language. Bruce Fulton is the inaugural holder of the Young-Bin Min Chair in Korean Literature and Literary Translation, Department of Asian Studies, University of British Columbia. He is presently a Visiting Professor in the Department of Korean Language and Literature at the University of Seoul.

바이링궐 에디션 한국 현대 소설 025

트렁크

2013년 6월 15일 초판 1쇄 발행
2023년 8월 14일 초판 2쇄 발행

지은이 정이현 | **옮긴이** 브루스 풀턴, 주찬 풀턴 | **펴낸이** 김재범
감수 브루스 풀턴 | **기획** 정은경, 전성태, 이경재
편집 정수인, 이은혜, 이윤정 | **관리** 박신영 | **디자인** 이춘희

펴낸곳 아시아 | **출판등록** 2006년 1월 31일 제319-2006-4호
주소 경기도 파주시 회동길 445(서울 사무소: 서울특별시 동작구 서달로 161-1, 3층)
전화 02.3280.5058 | **팩스** 070.7611.2505 | **홈페이지** www.bookasia.org
ISBN 978-89-94006-73-4 (set) | 978-89-94006-83-3 (04810)
값은 뒤표지에 있습니다.

Bi-lingual Edition Modern Korean Literature 025

In the Trunk

Written by Jeong Yi-hyun | **Translated by** Bruce Fulton and Ju-chan Fulton
Published by Asia Publishers
Address 445, Hoedong-gil, Paju-si, Gyeonggi-do, Korea
(Seoul Office:161-1, Seodal-ro, Dongjak-gu, Seoul, Korea)
Homepage Address www.bookasia.org | **Tel**. (822).3280.5058 | **Fax**. 070.7611.2505
First published in Korea by Asia Publishers 2013
ISBN 978-89-94006-73-4 (set) | 978-89-94006-83-3 (04810)

K-픽션 시리즈 | Korean Fiction Series

〈K-픽션〉 시리즈는 한국문학의 젊은 상상력입니다. 최근 발표된 가장 우수하고 흥미로운 작품을 엄선하여 출간하는 〈K-픽션〉은 한국문학의 생생한 현장을 국내외 독자들과 실시간으로 공유하고자 기획되었습니다. 〈바이링궐 에디션 한국 대표 소설〉 시리즈를 통해 검증된 탁월한 번역진이 참여하여 원작의 재미와 품격을 최대한 살린 〈K-픽션〉 시리즈는 매 계절마다 새로운 작품을 선보입니다.